THE NAKED LADY

※
———— ❦ ————

IAN WALLACE

ROARING BROOK PRESS
Brookfield, Connecticut

A Neal Porter Book

Copyright © 2002 by Ian Wallace

Published by Roaring Brook Press

A division of The Millbrook Press, 2 Old New Milford Road, Brookfield, Connecticut 06804

Library of Congress Cataloging-in-Publication Data

Wallace, Ian, 1950-

The naked lady / by Ian Wallace.

p. cm.

Summary: When a sculptor moves in to the farm next door, young Tom is inspired to become an artist.

[1. Artists—Fiction. 2. Sculpture—Fiction. 3. Farm life—Fiction.]   I. Title

PZ7.W1562 Nak 2002

[E]—dc21   2002023711

ISBN 0-7613-1596-9 (trade)   10 9 8 7 6 5 4 3 2 1

ISBN 0-7613-2660-X (library binding)   10 9 8 7 6 5 4 3 2 1

Printed in Hong Kong

First edition

For Pieter Doef

Stone Acre Farm had stood vacant and neglected for many years, when one day we noticed that someone had finally moved in.

"I hear he's an artist from the city," my dad said the next morning. "I bet he'll grow some colorful crops."

"I hope he's got a sweet tooth," my mom said as she handed me one of her prize-winning pies. "Be careful, Tom. Or there'll be raspberries in your sneakers instead of our neighbor's belly."

I cut through a cornfield, then climbed the wooded hill between our two farms. As I broke out of the trees, the sunlight was almost blinding. Through the glare I saw a giant woman dancing against the sky.

"SHE'S NAKED!" I gasped. The pie dropped out of my hand and hit the ground.

"She's not naked," a voice called back. "She's nude." I looked about. A man with a shiny head and a ponytail was coming toward me. "I'm Pieter," he said, and shook my hand.

"I'm Tom . . . Sims. From next door." I looked at my sneakers. "Mom's pie!" I untied the string and lifted the lid. Bright red juice oozed between the cracks in the crust and spilled over the bottom of the box. "She baked it to welcome you, and I broke it."

Pieter dipped a finger into the filling. "Broken is still delicious." He caught me staring at the naked lady. "That's 'Evangelina.' I sculpted her."

She was the most beautiful statue I'd ever seen. Not that I'd seen a real one before—except in books and magazines.

Back home, I told my parents about Pieter. With each detail, they laughed louder. "Now we know what that artist is going to grow," my dad said. "Naked ladies!"

That night, I climbed the hill again. To my surprise, I wasn't the

only one coming to see the naked lady. Pieter stepped into the sunset

carrying a bunch of wild irises. He placed them at her feet and

a coyote howled.

Sitting there, he looked like the loneliest man I'd ever seen. I wanted

to call out, but I felt so awkward, I just stood there. Finally, he

walked back down the hill.

The next morning, Dad and I were tilling a fallow field when Pieter came through the woods.

"That was one fine pie," he said. "Ate it in one go." He handed me my mom's plate. "Mr. Sims, I'm Pieter. I'm an artist, not a farmer. I plan on working only a few acres around my house. Would you be interested in working the rest? Any profit would be yours."

"You bet," my dad replied. "But I'd rather grow naked ladies than corn or soybeans," and he twirled around in a goofy spin.

"DAD!" I groaned.

But Pieter just laughed. "I could use some help tomorrow with a bit of planting. Can you give me a hand?"

When we arrived, Pieter was waiting inside his barn. Instead of bags of seed and bales of hay, it was filled with giant sculptures. Some of them had been carved from stone; others were made of wood. One by one, we loaded the sculptures onto a low wagon and secured them with ropes. Then, we attached the wagon to our tractor and headed into the fields. With each stop our load became lighter.

At the end of the day, Pieter's sculptures filled the fields. "There won't be a more awesome crop anywhere in the county this year," I said.

A week later my mom handed me another raspberry pie. "We have to take good care of Pieter," she said. "It must get pretty lonely over there."

I began to visit him often. Sometimes, I found him rocking on his porch. His eyes were red and swollen, and I thought he might have been crying. But when I watched him sculpt, he came alive with fire in his eyes.

One fall afternoon, he handed me my own box of pastels. He showed me how to hold the chalk. Then he taught me how to find details in the land, things I'd never noticed before. Sunlight on a scarecrow's face. Morning dew on dead leaves. Corn silk rustling in the wind.

I took my drawings home. My parents were so amazed that they hung the artwork on the kitchen wall. "That boy gets his talent from me," my dad said. My mother rolled her eyes.

The next Saturday, bales of hay were stacked in the center of the barn

floor. Nearby, a slab of clay sat on top of a tall wooden stand. "I need

a model," Pieter told me, "for a sculpture I've been thinking about.

You'd be a natural."

"Me?"

Pieter wielded a sculpting tool like a magician's wand. Then with one

quick stroke, he cut into the damp clay. "I'll make you famous, boy!"

"AWESOME!" I grabbed a pitchfork and leapt up onto the bales. I struck a pose that made him laugh. Then one more serious. And another more thoughtful.

"This one will be a working model. Later, I'll immortalize you in stone."

"What does im-mort-lize mean?"

"Captured forever just as you are today."

I looked myself over, then at the drawings on the walls. "Like Evangelina?"

Pieter smiled. "Yeah. Something like that."

I hesitated, then asked. "Who is she?"

Bits of clay fell away. "She was my wife . . . and my model . . . for forty-two years. And a dancer once, too. She passed away just before I moved here. Her ashes are buried beneath her sculpture." He cleared his throat. "Her grandfather built Stone Acre Farm with his own hands. Carved it out of rock and bush over a century ago."

Pieter worked in silence, cutting and shaping, molding and smoothing, even using a kitchen fork to create my hair. Gradually a boy with a pitchfork emerged. When he finished I couldn't believe what I saw. "It's me!"

Pieter looked out the barn door. "Sure as snow will come tonight."

By midnight the temperature fell, and the wind howled from the north. In its wake came a rare October snow. The next morning, our fields looked as if Pieter had painted them white. I ran all the way to Stone Acre Farm to see his crop of sculptures covered in glistening snow. As I stood in the center of the circle that he called "The Henge," I realized something I hadn't fully understood before. Pieter had lit a fire inside me. I wanted to be an artist, too.

When I entered the barn, he said, "Today, it's your turn to create whatever you'd like. An August raspberry pie. A ghostly Halloween pumpkin. Anything you want."

I didn't know where to start. I looked around the barn. The only sound came from the wind. I thought of Evangelina with snow swirling around her empty basket. In an instant, I knew what I wanted to make.

We made several rough drawings, working out the shapes, before cutting a piece of tin into long, narrow strips. Then we cut petal shapes. We painted each piece separately, coloring the strips green and the petals blue with yellow centers.

"They're beautiful," Pieter said. "Perfect."

Gathering up the bouquet, we climbed Evangelina's hill. The snow had melted beneath our feet, and the sun felt warm on my face. When we reached the statue, Pieter lifted me up and I set the wild irises inside her empty basket. I looked down over the hundred acres of Stone Acre Farm. Pieter's sculptures seemed as if they'd always been there, just like the corn and soybeans in my dad's fields and the raspberries on my mom's bushes.

*Y*ears later, after I'd grown up and left the farm for the city, I kept the promise I'd

made to myself that snowy morning in the center of "The Henge." I became an

artist, illustrating picture books for young people. The book you are holding is num-

ber nineteen. It is dedicated to Pieter, my first art teacher.